MERRY KISSMUS, LINCOLN!

BY: E.B. FLETCHER

ILLUSTRATIONS BY: DEBBIE TAYLOR

AuthorHouse™
1663 Liberty Drive
Bloomington, IN 47403
www.authorhouse.com
Phone: 1 (800) 839-8640

Because of the dynamic nature of the Internet, any web addresses or links contained in this
book may have changed since publication and may no longer be valid. The views expressed
in this work are solely those of the author and do not necessarily reflect the views of
the publisher, and the publisher hereby disclaims any responsibility for them.

Any people depicted in stock imagery provided by Getty Images are models,
and such images are being used for illustrative purposes only.
Certain stock imagery © Getty Images.

This book is printed on acid-free paper.

ISBN: 978-1-7283-3005-1 (sc)
ISBN: 978-1-7283-3006-8 (e)

Library of Congress Control Number: 2019915704

Print information available on the last page.

Published by AuthorHouse 10/02/2019

authorHOUSE®

To all those who rescue wonderful animals ...

♥

This book is dedicated to all the wonderful service
and military dogs in the world!

Some proceeds from the sale of this book go to the ASPCA.

Autumn was a pup who loved Christmas with all its trimmings – the lights, trees, cookies and presents. But, to a four year old tot still discovering the world, there was a lot Autumn didn't understand. Now Lincoln McCarthy, Attorney at Law, was her uncle, neighbor and protector. So, Autumn decided to pay him a call. *Maybe Uncle Carfee* (as she called him) *knows 'bout Kissmus.* "Uncle Carfee," Autumn called as she toddled about the house, "Where are *you?*"

"In here," Lincoln barked. "I'm workin' on a brief."

"Boo!" Autumn yapped bouncing into the room holding her bunny doll.

Lincoln, looked over his bi-focals, "Boo, yourself."

"You have a Kissmus twee!" Autumn gasped. She toddled over to the tree and stared up at the massive evergreen in all its twinkling wonder. Lincoln studied the inquisitive pup and smiled.

"Big Kissmus twee! I yike it!"

Lincoln came over and nuzzled her. "You like that tree, huh?"

"Yep. We got a Kissmus twee, too!" she said smiling widely.

"Well, just remember, no "*weedling*" on trees in the house," Lincoln grumbled.

"I 'member," Autumn snapped. "Evewybody knows you don't weedle on Kissmus twees!"

"Kissmus?" Lincoln quizzed.

"Yeah! You know ... the Kissmuses ... her's the wady who had the baby Cheese-etts."

Lincoln smiled at the inquisitive tyke. "Baby *Cheese-etts*?"

"Yeah, you know, baby Cheese-etts was born in a stapler, but I don't get it."

Lincoln chuckled, "I see," he said pulling a créche ornament from a nearby bough. "Tell me what you know about this ornament here," Lincoln directed watching the wide eyed tyke.

"Oh, that's the Kissmuses," Autumn said nodding, "See," she said pointing to each figure. "That's Mz Kissmus, and the baby Cheese-etts is in the manager … and that's Yosef."

"*Yosef?*" Lincoln puzzled.

"Yeah, him's Yosef Kissmus… Mewy's him's wife."

Lincoln's kind brown eyes softened, "Oh, I see … these are the Kissmuses, huh?"

"Yeah," Autumn said jostling her bunny doll. "Them the Kissmuses … dat's why evewybody says Mewy Kissmus 'cause Mewy was Cheese-etts' mommy, but God was his weal papa so, I guess Cheese-etts was kind'a adopted … Yosef said he'd be Cheese-etts' papa here on earf."

Lincoln adjusted his glasses, "I see," he said grabbing a Bible from his desk and pawing through it. "So, Autumn, tell me about this fella' here," he said pointing to one of the angels at the top of the ornament.

"Oh, that's an angle."

"An *angle?*"

"Yeah, there's tons of angles. They watch over us and the baby Cheese-etts."

"I see … who are the angles?"

"Oh, dims fly evewywhere and watch over the world. See, God tells 'em where to go.

They're him's messers."

"Messers?" Lincoln puzzled.

"Yeah, God's paper towels … they clean up messes … 'dem make things better!"

"Ahhh … so they do," Lincoln chuckled.

"You got a Bible. My mommy's got one, too," Autumn said smiling.

"Yes, she does. Your Grandma gave it to her. So, tell me, Autumn, what's this called?" Lincoln asked pointing to the manger.

"That's the manager in the stapler … see? It told the star to shine, like here on dis fing," Autumn said pawing at the star atop the créche ornament.

"How did that work?" Lincoln asked studying the inquisitive tot.

"WiFi," Autumn simply answered still clutching her bunny doll. "See, God told the star to shine and all the people in the fields came to see the baby Cheese-etts."

Lincoln scratched his head, "Who were the people in the fields?"

"The *shephewds*," Autumn answered rolling her eyes. "See, baby Cheese-etts is the *weal* shephewd but since he was just born, dey had to meet him. You sure you know dis stowy? Autumn asked eyeballing him.

"I thought I did," Lincoln sighed. "So, how did the shepherds get from the fields to baby Cheese- etts, ugh, **Jesus**?"

"Ubers, silly!" Autumn answered matter of factly.

"Oh, well of course they did ..." Lincoln chuckled tapping his paw on his forehead. Autumn gently took the créche ornament and turned it over in her paw. "Where are the Kissmus kings?"

"*Kings?*" Lincoln asked.

"Yeah, the Kissmuses had *thwee* **kings** that came to see 'em."

"Why did they have kings?" Lincoln asked placing his Bible on a nearby table.

"Dey hungwy ... all dose shephewds? They got buwgers for 'em," Autumn said proudly smiling for knowing scripture.

"*Burger* kings?"

"Yeah," Autumn nodded.

Lincoln settled himself into his wing chair watching the precious tyke. "So why did the baby need a stapler?"

"I don't *know!*" Autumn asked holding her paws upward with her head slightly titled. "*Why* Uncle Carfee? I don't get it!"

Lincoln chuckled, "Come here, Autumn," he said pulling the pup onto his lap. "We're going to read a story from the Book of Luke here in the Bible and we'll see how all this began with the what you call the Kissmuses. But, I must tell you, there is magic in the Christmas story."

"Like Kissmus snow?" Autumn asked settling beside him.

"Like snow, and forgiveness and love," said Lincoln as Autumn leaned against him.

"Does Kissmus magic work only at Kissmus time?"

"Oh no," Lincoln answered pulling the Bible onto his lap. "Christmas magic works all the year through. Yeah ... I've even seen it work on judges, juries and lawyers." Lincoln sighed settling into his favorite chair. He adjusted his glasses and then continued, "So you and bunny listen to the Christmas story as told by Luke:

King James Version; Luke 2 versus 1-35:

"And it came to pass in those days, that there went out a decree from Caesar Augustus, that all the world should be taxed. (And this taxing was first made when Cyrenius was governor of Syria.) And all went to be taxed, every one into his own city. And Joseph also went up from Galilee, out of the city of Nazareth, into Judaea, unto the city of David, which is called Bethlehem; (because he was of the house and lineage of David:) To be taxed with Mary his espoused wife, being great with child.

And so it was, that, while they were there, the days were accomplished that she should be delivered. And she brought forth her firstborn son, and wrapped him in swaddling clothes, and laid him in a manger; because there was no room for them in the inn. And there were in the same country shepherds abiding in the field, keeping watch over their flock by night. And, lo, the angel of the Lord came upon them, and the glory of the Lord shone round about them: and they were sore afraid. And the angel said unto them, Fear not: for, behold, I bring you good tidings of great joy, which shall be to all people. For unto you is born this day in the city of David a Saviour, which is Christ the Lord. And this shall be a sign unto you; Ye shall find the babe wrapped in swaddling clothes, lying in a manger. And suddenly there was with the angel a multitude of the heavenly host praising God, and saying, "Glory to God in the highest, and on earth peace, good will toward men."

And it came to pass, as the angels were gone away from them into heaven, the shepherds said one to another, Let us now go even unto Bethlehem, and see this thing which is come to pass, which the Lord hath made known unto us. And they came with haste, and found Mary, and Joseph, and the babe lying in a manger. And when they had seen it, they made known abroad the saying which was told them concerning this child. And all they that heard it wondered at those things which were told them by the shepherds. But Mary kept all these things, and pondered them in her heart. And the shepherds returned, glorifying and praising God for all the things that they had heard and seen, as it was told unto them. And when eight days were accomplished for the circumcising of the child, his name was called JESUS, which was so named of the angel before he was conceived in the womb.

And when the days of her purification according to the law of Moses were accomplished, they brought him to Jerusalem, to present him to the Lord; (As it is written in the law of the Lord, Every male that openeth the womb shall be called holy to the Lord;) and to offer a *sacrifice according to that which is said in the law of the Lord, A pair of turtledoves, or two young pigeons. And, behold, there was a man in Jerusalem, whose name was Simeon; and the same man was just and devout, waiting for the consolation of Israel: and the Holy Ghost was upon him. And it was revealed unto him by the Holy Ghost, that the Spirit into the temple: and when the parents brought in the child Jesus, to do for him after the custom of the law, then took he him up in his arms, and blessed God, and said, "Lord, now lettest thou thy servant depart in peace, according to thy word: For mine eyes have seen thy salvation, which thou hast prepared before the face of all people; A light to lighten the Gentiles, and the glory of thy people Israel. And Joseph and his mother marveled at those things which were spoken of him. And Simeon blessed them, and said unto Mary his mother, Behold, this child is set for the fall and rising again of many in Israel; and for a sign which shall be spoken against; Yea, a sword shall pierce through thy own soul also, that the thoughts of many hearts may be revealed."*

♥

Thanks be to God-EBF

CPSIA information can be obtained
at www.ICGtesting.com
Printed in the USA
BVHW020043131119
563624BV00006B/33/P

9 781728 330051